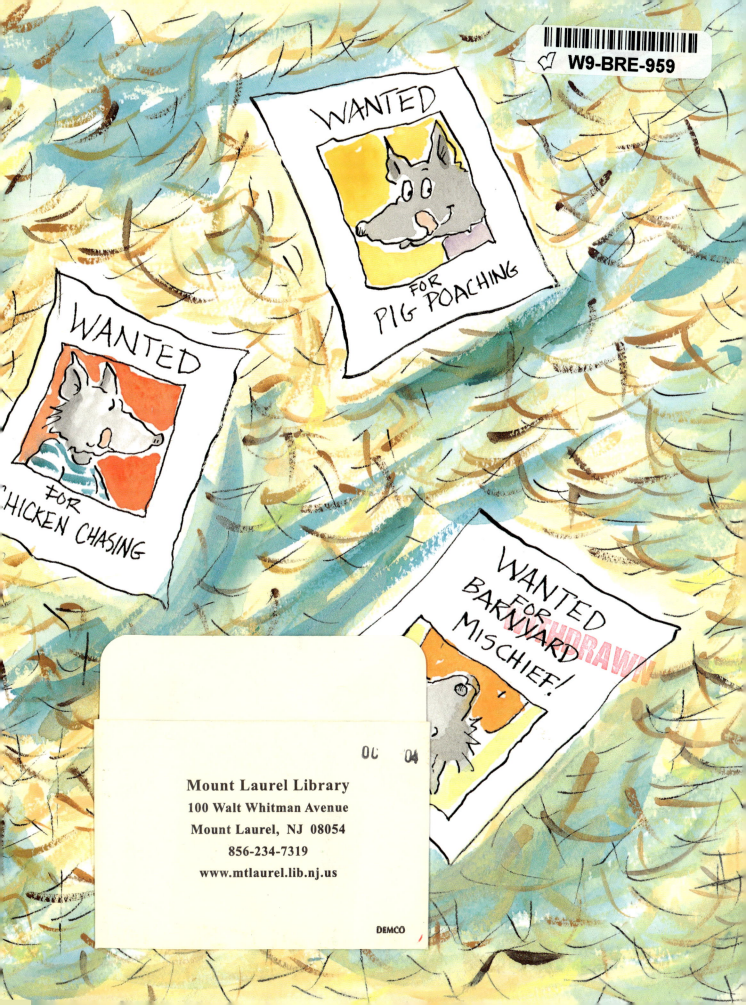

Clarion Books
a Houghton Mifflin Company imprint
215 Park Avenue South, New York, NY 10003
Copyright © 2002 by Eileen Christelow

The illustrations were executed in Holbein acrylic gouache and pen and ink.
The text was set in 18-point Centaur.

www.houghtonmifflinbooks.com

Printed in Singapore.

Library of Congress Cataloging-in-Publication Data
Christelow, Eileen.
Where's the big bad wolf? / Eileen Christelow.
p. cm.
Summary: Detective Doggedly, a pair of cows, and a sheep who looks very familiar are all
nearby each time three pigs get into trouble, but the big bad wolf is conspicuously absent.
ISBN 0-618-18194-6
[1. Dogs—Fiction. 2. Wolves—Fiction. 3. Domestic animals—Fiction.
4. Mystery and detective stories. 5. Humorous stories.] I. Title.

PZ7.C4523 Wh 2002
[E]—dc21 2001056189

TWP 10 9 8 7 6 5 4 3 2

Where's the Big Bad Wolf?

EILEEN CHRISTELOW

Clarion Books / New York

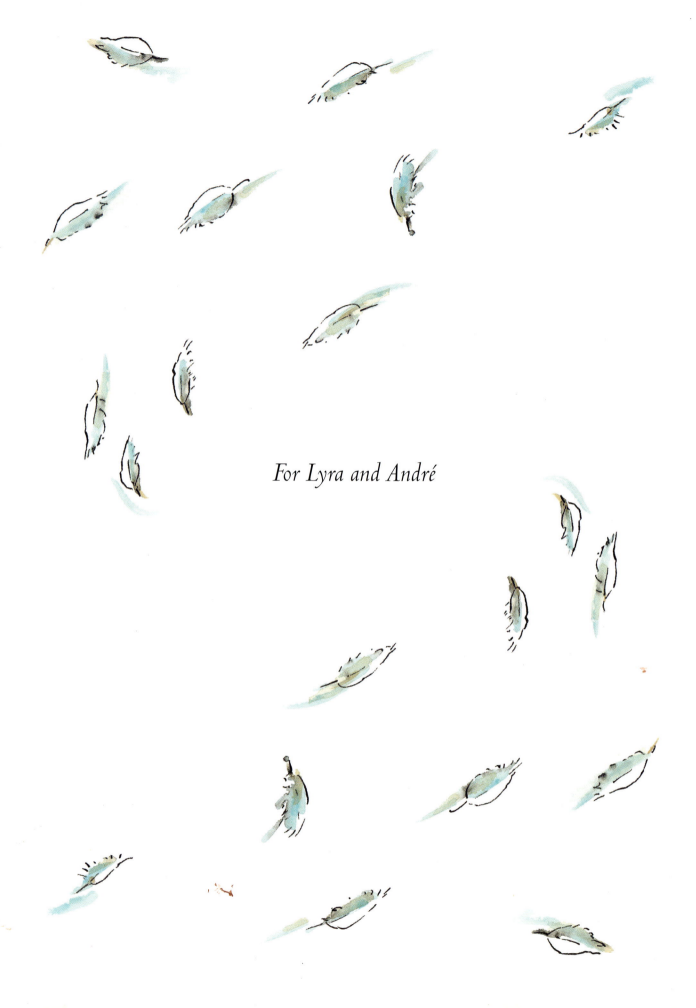

For Lyra and André

SQUAWK! SQUAWK! SQUAWK!

I'm Police Detective Phineas T. Doggedly.

Just call me Doggedly.

I catch low-down, no-good, chicken-chasing, pig-poaching rascals. It's an easy job because there's only one no-good rascal in this town.

That's the **Big Bad Wolf!**

Each time I catch the scoundrel, he promises, promises, *promises* he will be good forever from now on. Each time I hope it's true.

But that wolf just can't stay out of trouble.

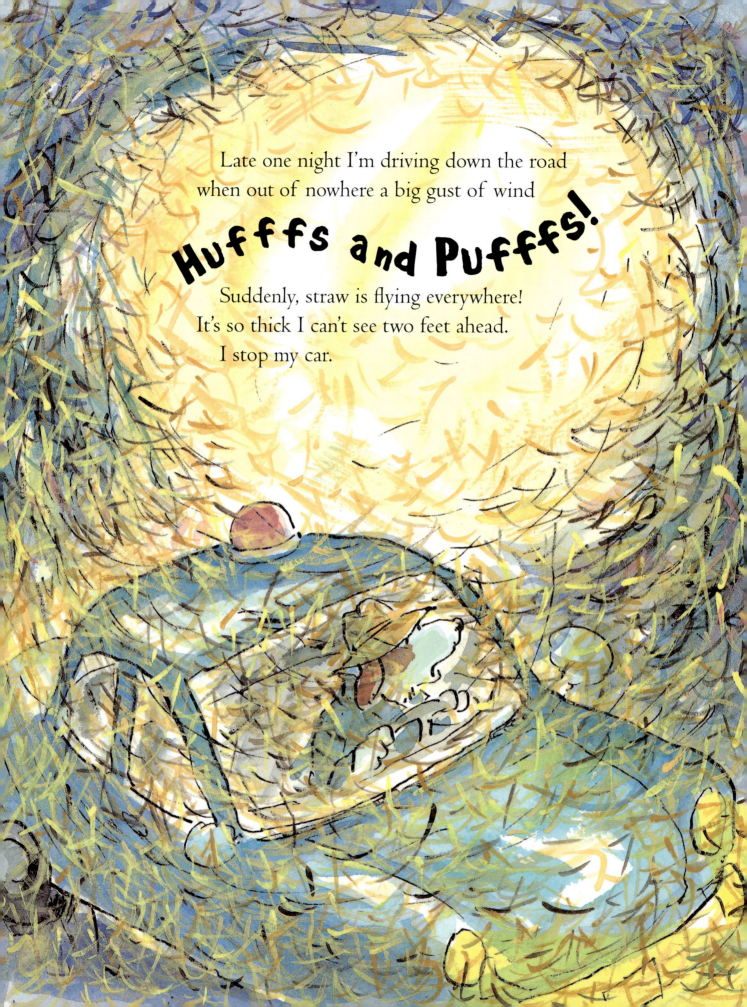

Late one night I'm driving down the road
when out of nowhere a big gust of wind

Hufffs and Pufffs!

Suddenly, straw is flying everywhere!
It's so thick I can't see two feet ahead.
I stop my car.

There's one last **puff**
and the straw settles.

I jump out of my car.
Eeee! Eeee! Eeee!
Sounds like pigs in distress!
Must be that pesky wolf, up to his old tricks!
I click on my flashlight.
Do I find the wolf?

No!

I find a **sheep**—pulling three little pigs from a pile of straw!

"What's going on?" I gasp. "Who are you?"

"I'm Esmeralda," says the sheep. "Good thing I happened to walk by—just in time to rescue these delectable little piggies!"

Just then the lights go on across the road.
Two elderly cows charge out the front door.
 "We warned those foolish pigs!" they bellow.
"But would they listen to a bunch of old cows?
No! They listened to that silly sheep and they
built a flimsy straw house. And look what
happened!"
 "A tornado blew it down!" squeal the pigs.

"Tornado?" I say. "More likely it was that good-for-nothing, huffing, puffing bag of wind the Big Bad Wolf who blew your house down. He's well known for such mischief."

"That's right!" shout the cows. "He's probably hiding in these bushes."

"Oh, no!" shrieks Esmeralda. "Wolves are so scary! I'm getting out of here!"

The sheep hightails it out of there fast as greased lightning.

The rest of us search through the bushes for that no-account, pig-poaching wolf. But it looks like he got away!

"You'd better find him, Doggedly," say the cows.

"You look after the piggies," I say. "I'll catch the scoundrel if it takes all night."

I finally find the wolf—at home.
"Whatever it is, I didn't do it!" he groans. "I've been much too sick with flu-like symptoms."
"An unlikely story," I say. "Considering your pig-poaching past."

But I have to admit, the wolf doesn't look like
he could blow out a birthday candle, much less a
flimsy straw house.

"I'm being framed!" the wolf wheezes.
"There must be another wolf trying to poach
on my territory."

"If there's another wolf around here, my
mother's a poodle!" I growl.

Something funny is going on. I just can't
quite put my paw on what it is.

The next morning I snoop around looking for another wolf.
That crazy sheep, Esmeralda, is giving the three little pigs
more house-building advice.

"Build a stick house," she says. "It's so easy!"

"Easy—but flimsy!" warn the cows.

"Easy sounds good," say the pigs.

"Just plain foolish," grumble the cows. "Where did that daffy sheep come from, anyway?"

"Beats me," I say. "Although she looks kind of familiar . . ."

By late evening the little pigs are fast asleep in their new stick house.

I park my car behind a bush and wait.

"It's a mighty flimsy house," I mutter to myself. "That windbag wolf might blow it down with one huff and a puff. But this time I'll nab him!"

Esmeralda is out for a walk. Otherwise, the street is quiet. I sure could use a nap!

HOME FOR

17

Huff-f-f!
Puff-f-f!
Thump!
Crash!

I suddenly wake up!

Sticks are flying!
Pigs are squealing!

Eeee! Eeee! Eeee!

"Pigs in distress!" I gasp. "It's the wolf!"
I jump out of my car.
I click on my flashlight . . .

And there's Esmeralda!

"Hi!" she says. "Lucky I was walking by again—just in time to rescue these tender little piggies."

"Where's that wolf?" I growl.

Just then the elderly cows race outside.

"Enough is enough!" they cry. "With all this huffing, puffing, crashing, and thumping, we can't get any sleep! It's time these foolish pigs learned a thing or two!"

They march the little pigs inside.

21

They put the pigs to bed and read them a well-known bedtime story. I'd like to hang around and listen, but I need to find that huffing, puffing wolf.

I search all over. I finally find him in the hospital.
"Don't think you can hide out here!" I snarl.
"Doggedly!" says the nurse. "Leave this poor wolf alone! He came in this morning with mysterious flu-like symptoms. Most likely he'll be here for days."
There's something strange going on! I just can't quite put my paw on what it is.

The next day I snoop around again.

The little pigs are building a new house—with bricks.

"No! No! No!" groans Esmeralda. "Build a *cardboard* house. It's so much easier."

"Easy to build, easy to blow down," say the little pigs.

After many days of hard work, the little pigs move into their new brick house.

"The big bad wolf can't blow this house down!" say the elderly cows.

But I'm not so sure he won't try.

That night after the pigs are in bed, I park my car behind some bushes and wait. The elderly cows bring out tea and cookies and wait with me.

Pretty soon we hear,

Huff-ff-ff!
Puff-ff-ff!

Gasp! Gasp!

Huff- gasp!

Crash!   Ouch!

Huff! Pant!

Bang . . . ouch . . gasp . . . pant!

"The wolf!" I growl.
"Let's get him!" bellow the cows.
We jump out of the car.
We click on our flashlights and race across the road.
What do we find?

The little pigs and their house are safe and sound. But there's no wolf!

"Where's that wolf?" bellow the cows.

Off in the distance I see a shadowy figure, wearing a red skirt, running down the road. It looks like Esmeralda.

"There's something strange going on," I say. "And I'm going to find out what it is."

I chase down the road after Esmeralda. I'm about to pass the hospital when I catch sight of her red skirt disappearing through a window. I screech to a halt and follow.

You'll never guess who I find!

The Big Bad Wolf!!!

He's gasping, wheezing, groaning, and moaning.
"I can't imagine what happened," says the nurse.
"He's all huffed and puffed out!"
That's when I put two and two together.
"This no-good, pig-poaching, huffing, puffing
wolf-in-sheep's-clothing is under arrest!" I growl.

The Big Bad Wolf has to spend a few sorry days
in jail. When I let him out, he promises, promises,
promises he will be good forever. This time I really
hope he's learned his lesson.

As for the three little pigs, they're planting a vegetable garden. They're getting lots of advice from a **horse** who just moved to town.

There is something mighty strange about that horse, but I just can't put my paw on what it is.

33